# A HOLIDAY LIFT

## CORINNE MICHAELS

*A Holiday Lift*

Copyright © 2020 Corinne Michaels
All rights reserved.
ISBN e-book: 978-1-942834-61-8
ISBN print: 978-1-942834-62-5

This book is a work of fiction. Names, characters, places, and incidents either are products of the author's imagination or are used fictitiously. Any resemblance to actual events or locales or persons, living or dead, is entirely coincidental and beyond the intent of the author or publisher.

Cover Design: Chelle Bliss
Editing: Ashley Williams, AW Editing
Proofreading: Michele Ficht

*Brendan, you are my Christmas.*

# PREFACE

My Dearest Reader,

When I wrote A Holiday Lift two years ago, I was so excited because holiday stories are my favorite. It's where we get to meet new characters or revisit old ones. I wanted to write a short story where we get the magic of Christmas. Something that was still very me (but not as angsty) and showed us that amazing things can happen around this time of year.

Holly and Dean did just that.

Of course, I could help but put the angst in because I think there's seriously something wrong with me, but that's what makes it fun, right?

This story was originally free in the Naughty and Nice anthology. However, when Passionflix optioned it for a holiday quickie, I found myself nostalgic and completely in love with this story again.

So, on the flight home from filming, I couldn't stop my mind from needing to tell more. Hence *this* edition of it.

If you have already read it a few years ago, you'll recognize the beginning, but there is a LOT of new story here. Dean and Holly's story took a pause, but they're back now and I wanted you see just what happened to them after the end wasn't really the end anymore.

It's short.

It's sweet.

It's Christmas and magic and all I kept thinking was … man, I love the holidays and hope you do too!

Love,

Corinne

#  Holly

"**S**hit!" I say as I fall to the ground half inside the elevator and half in the hall. Humiliated, I force my eyes open, only to see a pair of caramel-colored dress shoes and my dignity right there before me. Seriously, this is the worst day of my life.

This morning I found out the pitch I was going to give *after* the new year was moved to tomorrow, and then I found out it wasn't Yamina who I was pitching against. Nope, it was the only person in the office who could actually kick my ass and get the account.

But that is nothing to me as I lie there in a stupid skirt for all the office to see.

"Here, let me help you." A deep voice I'd know

anywhere fills my ears a second before an offered hand drops into my line of sight.

*Please, God, let this not be happening.*

I lift my eyes and find that not only is it happening but also it's happening in front of the hottest man in the building, my new enemy, the man I slept with a week ago. He's also the man I have deep feelings for but pretend not to.

"I'm fine," I say, trying to stop the heat from flooding my cheeks.

The doors close on my body, and I attempt to maneuver, but I can't get up without showing all my glory.

"Holly," Dean Pritchard says. "Give me your hand."

Not wanting to make this any worse than it already is, I put my hand in his. "Thanks." He helps me up, smirking at me, but at least he isn't laughing.

"Are you okay?"

Like he cares. If he did, he would've called. He wouldn't have ignored me since our drunken night of unbelievable sex. I wouldn't have been invisible. "I'm fine. Other than being embarrassed."

I smooth my skirt down, knowing that it lifted enough for everyone to see my bare ass.

"It looked like it hurt."

Only my pride. "Press two please," I say, desperate to get off the topic.

The last thing I want is to stand here and talk about the awkward fall.

"I never pegged you for going commando."

"Not like you haven't seen it already," I say, adding another reason why I should get a do-over for today.

I had underwear on when I left the house, but they ripped when I went to the bathroom because I'm the biggest klutz ever and put my high heel through the crotch. That was ten minutes ago. Oh, how I wish I had a time machine.

"True." He grins. "Still an interesting new tidbit about you."

*Yeah, I'm just full of them.*

"Whatever, did you get the proposal done? I know it was last minute for you." I'm still smoothing my clothes out as the elevator door shuts with me safely inside this time.

"I did. You?"

*Nope.*

"Yes."

"Good. May the best man win."

"Oh, I plan to."

Dean laughs. "We'll see. Maybe the winner buys the other some scotch?"

My eyes narrow. That was what we'd been drinking the night we got drunk and screwed against his office door, floor, and desk. "That will *never* happen again."

Well, it will in my dreams because it has six times since then, but there's no way I'll admit that. That night was a huge mistake, but it was the best sex of my life.

He chuckles. "If you say so."

I turn away, wishing the elevator would hurry up. My office is on the fifty-eighth floor. While the ride doesn't typically feel like a million years, right now, I feel like I'm dying a slow death.

"Doesn't this thing move faster?" The music isn't helping. There's nothing about this being the best time of the year.

The holidays do nothing but remind me that I'm alone. Every time I look at decorations, I try not to remember how much Troy would enjoy being out there on Thanksgiving night, stringing up the lights. He proposed to me on Christmas three years ago.

It was the perfect proposal. The one that girls around the world swoon over because it was just that romantic. And it was.

We were standing in our living room, dancing to "Silent Night," and the fire was burning, giving me that perfect glow. Our beautifully lit tree was sending a shimmery white glow around the room as he held me in his arms. He leaned down, kissed my lips, and told me he wanted to spend every Christmas just like that.

Then he dropped to his knee, took out the ring, and I sobbed while nodding yes over and over.

I believed that Santa was real and he brought me the best gift ever.

A year later, when he decided he didn't love me anymore, I learned Santa was a fraud and that the fat man had been fired, was on a diet, and shaved off his beard.

Troy ruined my favorite holiday, and of course, I don't get to pretend it doesn't exist because it's almost my birthday. Therefore, Christmas is forever a celebration. Blah.

"Are you heading to the boss's office?" Dean asks.

"No, you?"

"Yeah, I have a meeting today since I'm leaving for California. I figured it was better to do the pitch now."

Oh, sure, he can go first, wow them, and then I'll really be out. No way. I'm not going to let him weasel his way into this account like he always does.

Well, weasel is a strong word. He's smart, cunning, and actually good at his job, which is just one more reason to hate him.

Oh, and he is *really* fucking good in bed.

Like, really good.

"That's totally unfair—" The elevator slams to a stop, jerking up and down, forcing me to almost topple over. If it weren't for Dean's strong arms wrapping around me and stopping my second fall of the day, I probably would have.

The lights flicker and then the small emergency light goes on.

Great. This is just what I needed.

Fucking holidays.

## 2

"**A**re you all right?" he asks for the second time in the last five minutes.

My heart is racing from the punch of adrenaline and a bit from his cologne that fills my nose as I draw a deep breath. Damn, why does he have to smell so good?

"Yes, thank you—again." I hate that, out of all the people in the building, this has to happen in front of Dean. Him constantly helping me up and catching me before I fall is so freaking contradictory. He's the first guy I've thought about since Troy, I thought maybe he felt something for me, but then he brushed me off as if I were nothing.

How can he be both people in my head?

How can he be so sweet one minute but then ignore me completely the next?

It's not as if he didn't know about my past. In fact, that night we spoke about it. I told him about how this holiday would be hard because of my ex. We talked about work, life, our lives since both our breakups. It was great, but then he acted like I was nothing.

Although, that's what we said before it happened.

I'm attempting to convince myself that was exactly what we both agreed to and he's just keeping his word, but . . . I hoped.

I came in the next day, smiling with a coffee for him. He walked right past me and hasn't said a word about what happened since then.

It's incomprehensible to me that I finally let myself feel something other than rage toward a man, only to be . . . ignored after sex.

"Of course." He smiles and presses the call button.

"Hello?" A man on the other end replies.

"Hi, this is Dean Pritchard and we're stuck, can you get us going please?"

"Yes, is everyone okay?"

Dean looks back at me. "Yes, Holly Brickman and I are in here, but we're not moving and the emergency lights are on."

The man clears his throat. "Yes, we're aware. There was a power outage due to the heavy snow, and unfortunately, it looks like a transformer blew, leaving the whole block out of power. The generator is broken as well, found that out late last night when we tested it, but as soon as we can get you both out, we will. Okay?"

"How long?" I yell. "I need to know!"

Dean looks back at me since the button wasn't down and the guy on the other line couldn't exactly hear me. He then presses it and speaks. "How long do you think that could be?"

"Not sure, sir. I'll get back to you when I can. We're working on getting you guys out just as fast as we can."

"Great," I mutter. "Another thing to add to why I hate the damn holidays. And old buildings."

Dean shakes his head, and his brows furrow. "Why the hell do you hate the holidays? No one hates this time of year."

"Well, I have a ton of reasons. Snow. Santa. Stupid men. Power outages. Elevators being stuck. The list really goes on . . ."

He removes his suit jacket, revealing his tight shirt that hugs all the right places. I try not to remember how it felt to have him moving above me as I gripped those arms—I fail. The memories of that night flood me. The scotch, taste of his lips, and how amazing every moment we spent together was.

"Santa?" Dean asks. "You hate Santa?"

"Yeah, him and his stupid list, which apparently I landed on the naughty side of two years ago. My gift was to get dumped. It really changed my feelings on all things holiday related."

"Ahh." He nods. "Yes, now I get it."

When it happened, it wasn't something I was quiet about. Not that I could've been if I wanted to be. I sobbed all the time. I swear I should've carried around a sign that said: Caution Slippery When Wet. With the amount of tears I cried, I left a trail. Plus, half my company was invited to the wedding that would've been seven days from today. Sending out the I-just-got-dumped email was super fun.

"Not my favorite time of year thanks to a certain someone."

"You mean that idiot of an ex you were engaged to?"

"Please . . . I don't want to talk about him." Especially not with him.

"Understood." He nudges me. "I could help you forget him again."

I roll my eyes. "No thanks. Besides, I don't really think about him at all."

*I'm too busy thinking about you.*

"I'm glad to hear that. He wasn't good enough for you anyway." He shrugs and folds his jacket in half and then sits on the floor beside it. He doesn't speak as he extends his hand for me to sit there.

"Why is that?"

Dean cracks his neck, looking a little uncomfortable as he offers a simple, "Because."

I laugh and cross my arms. "Well, that clears all that up."

"Why don't you sit, Holly? We could be in here for a while."

"Thank you." I sit on the jacket, crossing my ankles in front of me since I'm not wearing panties. "I'm sorry I was being sort of bitchy. Troy does that to me."

"Don't be. I don't exactly like talking about my ex either."

I nod. "Yeah, they aren't usually a great topic."

"Okay, so let's move to neutral ground. We could talk about us," he suggests with a hint of mischief. "Or we can just be quiet . . ."

Oh, the possibilities for that suggestion are as endless as they are unlikely. And with as low on the list as talking to Dean about Tony is, talking to him about what happened is even lower.

"Can we keep talking? Please? Just not about any of the aforementioned things."

"Okay then, what about your pitch, do you want to practice?"

I laugh. No freaking way am I going to tell him my pitch. "I'd rather swallow nails than go there."

"Is it because you aren't confident?"

I raise my brow. "No, it's because I would rather not give you an edge."

Or because I don't have it done and don't want him to know that.

"I don't need an edge, babe. I plan to kick your ass."

"Really? You've had a whole a day to get your presentation together, and you think you're going to win?"

Dean's eyes narrow and he leans close. "You hate Christmas. This is all about why the holidays are the best time of the year. You're sort of the poster child for who not to hire."

"I can fake it."

"Ahh, but I know the real thing. You're exquisite when you're not faking it."

I scoff. "You do *not* get to bring up my orgasms in a business conversation."

He chuckles that deep laugh that does things to my girly parts. "Sorry, I couldn't resist. Why would you even want this account? You'll have to practically pretend you live in Santa's workshop and you're his bitch."

Admitting this will make me sound so stupid, but it's the truth. "I want to love the holidays again. I want to remember the magic and smile when I put my tree up again. I thought . . . I thought that maybe this would help."

Dean's hand rests on mine. "You shouldn't have ever had to feel that way, Holls."

I shake my head, not wanting to spill any more of my crazy in front of him. "Next topic."

"All right, why don't you tell me why you ran off last week?"

He's like a beacon for topics I want to avoid. "Jesus Cringle! Can't we talk about the damn weather instead of the worst topics possible?"

"Cringle?"

I know . . . I'm a dork. My mother used to say it when she was mad instead of cursing, so I can't help it. "It's my version of Christ."

His smile brightens the dim space. "Adorable."

My stomach clenches, and I look away. Is he calling me adorable or does he think the word is adorable? Either way, it shouldn't matter. Dean and I are nothing, and we're about to battle for this account where I will make everyone believe the holidays are nothing but joy because I'm a professional.

"Do you think we could talk about something else?"

"You want to talk, I pick what we talk about. You just mentioned the sex, I'd like to find out what the hell had you bolt like that." His eyes are the most beautiful shade of green.

"There's nothing to talk about." Really, they are almost hypnotic in their stupid, deep color.

"I disagree."

I tuck my hair behind my ear and sigh. "I didn't bolt. It was late, we clearly hadn't been thinking, and I didn't want to make things awkward. I got my coat, and when I looked back, your office door was closed and the lights were off."

Dean pushes a piece of my hair that fell from its place and shakes his head. "I was waiting for you, Holls. I heard you talking to yourself."

My eyes bulge. "What?"

"I heard you say this was a mistake and that you wished you never saw me again."

It was what I said to myself to make whatever happened next okay. "I . . ."

"I get it, you were scared."

My heart races as I stare into his eyes. "Of what?"

He leans in closer. "Me."

He does scare me. I'm scared because my brain clearly stops functioning when he's around and I will end up saying something dumb or making a bigger fool of myself. I'm scared that I'll spend another Christmas/birthday wondering what's wrong with me. I'm terrified that, once again, I'll be left alone.

"What do you want me to say?"

"The truth for starters."

"The truth is that we had sex and then you never called."

He shakes his head. "You wanted me to call?"

I don't know what I wanted. "No. Yes. I just . . . let's not do this, okay?"

"There's a reason I didn't call. Contrary to what you think, Holly, I'm not a dick."

"Regarding work, you are . . ."

"Okay, maybe with that."

I sigh, which is a bit of a laugh, and so does he. We all know that Dean is ruthless when it comes to his job. He started at the bottom and has fought his way up. With the project manager being transferred to the Phoenix office, there will be a very big promotion up for grabs here. His name plaque might as well be on the office door already.

"What are you heading to California for?" I ask, hoping we can talk about anything other than the sex and lack of calls.

He releases a heavy breath. "My family lives there,

15

and I'm going home for the holidays and staying for a while after."

"What do you mean a while?"

Dean rubs the back of his head. "My mother has been begging me to stay closer to home. I guess she misses me or something." He laughs. "So, I figure maybe I'll see what's out there and interview a bit. I don't know. It depends on the promotion here too . . ."

My heart falls, and I have the strongest urge to cry. I don't want him to leave, which is stupid and scary. I wonder if the cold air does something to my brain? It would add another item to the list of things I hate about December.

"Oh." Is all I seem to get out.

"Oh?"

"I guess I'm surprised you'd even think of leaving Chicago. Especially since you seem to be the golden boy here. It didn't even occur to me that you'd transfer out there or leave the company when we all know you're going to get the promotion."

Dean shakes his head. "You're the one they keep going to for all these pitches. We both know that the promotion is yours."

I jerk my head back. He's crazy. "Please, you win every account you pitch for. It's why we all hate you."

"You included?" he asked as he clearly fought to keep the smirk off his lips.

I wish I did. I wish he wasn't so damn good looking. I wish I didn't dream of him every night and didn't find his confidence so damn attractive. I would give anything for the simmer of feelings I have for him to die out. That would really make it easier.

"Wouldn't you like to know?"

"I would, in fact."

"Well, too bad."

He clutches his chest. "You wound me, and at Christmas time?"

"Please. You're just fine. Back to the job thing . . ."

"There's nothing definite, it's just a possibility. I'm really just appeasing my family."

I understand that. My mother is an overbearing crazy person. She was over last night, telling me how I needed to get my life together. It's been almost two years, and she's worried I'm going to die alone with a gaggle of cats.

"No matter what happens, I hope it's what you want to happen, even if it means you have to move."

Dean takes his other hand and laces our fingers together. "What if I told you that I hope I don't find anything?"

"Why would you say that?"

His thumb grazes the top of my hand. "Because I like someone here."

Our eyes meet, and my heart begins to race. "You

do? Who?" I ask, really hoping it's my name out of his mouth.

Ugh. I shouldn't want that, but the other night changed something inside me.

"Wouldn't you like to know?" He finally lets his smirk out as he throws my words back in face.

"You're such an ass. Maybe I don't really want to know. Maybe I do. Maybe I don't care who you like because, if you cared, you'd tell me," I counter.

Dean turns, his eyes meet mine, and there's no mincing words this time. "I like you, Holly. I like you, and the other night wasn't just some random drunken fling."

I shake my head to clear the fog of emotions that start to cloud my vision. If he liked me, he would've called. He would've done something to let me know instead of forcing himself to say it because we're trapped in an elevator. Hell, he probably only said it *because* we are stuck in this elevator.

Still, my heart begins to flutter. "You don't have to say nice things because we're stuck in an elevator. I'm a big girl. I can handle a one-night stand or whatever we're calling it."

"I'm not saying it for any of those reasons. I'm saying it because I mean it. It wasn't that I didn't want to call you, it was that I knew you didn't want me to call you. I heard you say it was a mistake. Then the day after we slept together, I found out I was pitching against you, and I wasn't exactly sure how the hell we were going to pick up from that. Most of all, I wanted to call. I wanted so fucking badly to see you again."

Why does he make me feel gooey inside? Why do I want to lunge at him and kiss him? Why can't I shut down these feelings when I know all he wants is this job?

Because I'm crazy, that's why.

I get to my feet, needing the leverage and distance. Not that there's anywhere to go when I'm stuck in an elevator, but still.

I look at Dean, wondering if what he's saying is true. "Dean . . ."

"No, don't say anything to try to make what I said a lie."

"Why do the holidays seem to bring around so much confusion and hurt with men?" I mutter.

I used to love Christmas. It was truly the most magical time, but the bad memories always take hold and remove the joy I used to feel. There are a thousand good memories to that one horrible one, but I know I'll only ever really remember how much it hurt when he left me. This year probably hurts more than when he left. This Christmas Eve would've been my wedding day. On this holiday, I'll eat another birthday cake instead of a wedding one.

I look to the ceiling. "Seriously, could they get the damn power started so I can hide? I'm completely hopeless when it comes to relationships."

Dean gets to his feet, crowding me, making me feel everything because I can't escape him. He pushes away a piece of my blonde hair that fell in my eye. "There's still hope for you, Holly."

I turn my head and bite my lip. "I don't think so."

He grips my chin so I'm forced to look at him. Dean's eyes are intense, and there's a layer of fear just lying beneath the surface. "You are not hopeless. You had a guy who didn't see how great you are, who didn't deserve you. You don't see what you have around you or in front of you."

## 3

# ▲ Dean ▲

*I* don't know what I'm doing saying any of this.

Maybe it's because her blue eyes turn dull when she's hurting and I want to brighten them again. She's the most beautiful woman I've ever seen. Almost from the day I met her, I've battled with having feelings for her, knowing she was with someone else and I couldn't have her.

Then when that dickhead of a fiancé she had left her, I fucking threw a party.

I hated him. He was a tool who never deserved her.

Then after he left her, she needed time. Her pain was evident as she struggled.

There were times I tried to make her laugh, smile,

forget about him, and over the last few months . . . she did.

We started working on a pitch for a new vitamin type drink. Long nights with takeout in the office made it impossible not to fall harder for her.

I spent so long pretending that it was just lust, but I can't do that anymore. Now that I've had her, I don't ever want to let her go again.

"I don't understand . . ."

My hand lifts, gently touching her cheek. "What don't you understand?"

She tries to step back farther, but there's nowhere to go. "This! Us. Why would you say all this when you're going to California and aren't sure if you'll find another job or come back? Do you want to give me another reason to hate Christmas?"

The last thing I want to do is hurt her more. I tried to get out of going home. I planned to talk to her this week, see her and explain that I don't think the other night was a mistake. My whole goal was to make her Christmas something special. Take her out on a real date, show her that it isn't the holidays that are shit— it is the dickhead she was with.

"No. That definitely is not my intention."

Her hand presses at my chest, but I don't move. I can't let her get away before she knows how I feel. "Then what are you trying to do?"

"I'm trying to make you see."

"See what?"

Instead of answering her with words, I kiss her. My mouth is hard against hers, and she freezes. Kissing Holly is everything I remember and more. The hand that was trying to push me away is now grasping at my shirt. Her lips go from rigid to soft as she kisses me back.

I feel her fighting herself, though. When we were together last week, she was completely uninhibited. She let go, and God, it was beautiful.

"Stop thinking," I say. Our lips just brushing. "Stop trying to make these crazy things in your head reality. Stop pulling away."

"Stop talking," she counters.

Her hand snakes around the back of my head, and she kisses me this time.

My palms travel down her slender body, wanting to feel her skin but knowing she doesn't trust me not to hurt her. I need her to see I'm nothing like the guy she believes I am.

She breaks the kiss and tries to calm her breath.

Her blue eyes are filled with passion and confliction.

I run my fingers across her cheek, and she smiles.

"Do you have any idea how many times I've imagined kissing you in this elevator?"

"Yeah?"

The most beautiful shade of pink paints her cheeks. "I've liked you for a while, but Dean, we work together, and this California thing . . ."

"I'll come back," I vow. "If you tell me there's a chance, I'll come back."

# 4

The sound of my heart pounding is so loud that I'm sure he can hear it. "There's more than a chance."

I can't believe I just said it, but I'm tired of fighting the feelings I have.

I care about him, and I've been fooling myself by saying anything else. He's sweet, caring, and if he left, I would forever wonder.

Dean is the opposite of anyone I've ever been with, and I think that's a good thing.

"There is?"

He can't leave without knowing, because I want him to come back. Even if it means I never get another account again. Well, maybe not that much, but still.

My breathing is shallow as I tell him everything that's in my heart. "I care about you, Dean. I have for a long time. I know what you overheard, but none of it was true. I only said it because bad things happen around this time of year and I wanted to protect myself. I wanted to believe we could be together, but then everything just felt so . . . scary."

I give him my truth because I trust him with it. He's never lied to me, and he's always done anything he could to make me smile.

When I was broken, Dean somehow always made getting up and coming to work a little less painful. He never pushed me, but now there's no going back.

"I'm going to make you love Christmas again, Holls. I'm going to show you that Santa, snow, the music, and all things are full of joy."

I shake my head, both telling him no and denying the claim to myself. "How do you plan to do that?"

He presses his lips to mine, and I push my body against his. "By reminding you that it's how we got together. Because if that stupid snowstorm hadn't knocked the power out during the time of year when Santa comes and if the music weren't playing in our office that night, we wouldn't have joy. We wouldn't have finally stopped pretending these feelings between us were really happening."

My lips turn up, and I play with the hair on the

back of his neck. "I think this could've happened in the summer."

Dean nods with a shrug. "Maybe, but I believe there's something magical in the air that makes it so we all can't help but accept what comes our way."

Before I can say another word, the elevator jerks and we're moving. I go to step away, but Dean holds me tight. Then the door opens and there are three people standing there, looking at the two of us in each other's arms.

"Well, seems you guys are doing just fine," an older gentleman says before letting out a low chuckle.

"Yeah, I think we are," Dean says as he steps back and grabs his jacket from the floor.

For the first time in a long time, I think I am too. It may not have been the way I wanted to spend an hour of my time, but it ended up being the best hour of my life.

He extends his hand, and I take it.

"You two have to kiss," the older man says, and I finally get a look at him.

He's a heavy man with a white beard. He looks exactly like . . . Santa. There's a glimmer in his eyes as though he already knows that's exactly what we were doing in that elevator.

"What?" I say.

He points to the ceiling right outside of the elevator door. "Mistletoe."

"Oh."

"It's bad luck," Santa look-alike says. "Plus, it's the holidays. You never know what can happen if you believe. Do you believe, Holly?"

I look at Dean and smile. "Yeah, I do. It's really the best time of year."

Dean grins and presses his lips to mine, reminding me that anything can happen during the holidays if you just have faith.


**WHAT WAS PREVIOUSLY "THE END" . . .**


*THANK you for reading this short story of A Holiday Lift. I was reminded of how much I loved writing Dean and Holly after watching Passionflix film it that I knew I needed to go in and give more. I wanted answers to my own questions and to see where they went. So . . . did Dean show Holly that this time of year is the best? Read and find out.*

## 5

~TWO YEARS LATER~

"*D*ean! Can you please help me?" I yell from my rather precarious spot on the stepstool.

He rushes into the living room, his eyes wide. "What are you doing?" I hear him say as he reaches to stop the stool from teetering on two legs.

"The angel was crooked," I explain as if it should be obvious.

"Regardless, you shouldn't be climbing up there."

I roll my eyes. "It's fine."

"And if you fell?"

I step down, my hand touching his cheek. "You'd catch me."

The anger deflates a little from him. "Not if I didn't know you were falling."

"I have faith."

The last few months have been crazy. Yes, the holidays are always busy at the agency, but with the two of us being promoted in different departments, our hours have been ridiculous, leaving us to struggle to find time to see each other.

Dean got the promotion to the new department, and after my boss quit, I was given his spot. It made us dating much easier and people asked far fewer questions.

Not to mention, everyone at work considered us a foregone conclusion. Apparently, we weren't very subtle.

"I've missed you," he says as he wraps his arms around me.

"It's been so hard with the new accounts we've gotten," I say, loosening his tie. "Do you have everything settled with your new hire?"

He groans. "Not even close. She's ambitious, which is great, but she's reckless."

"You'll get her sorted out," I reassure him.

"It would be much easier if she weren't the owner's daughter."

I tap my hand on his chest with a grin. "Yeah, that does suck for you."

Dean laughs before giving me a brief kiss. "Still, it's a good thing we're busy."

"I know, but we'll get a reprieve after the new year, right?"

He sighs deeply. "I doubt that I will."

"Why?"

"Because I just got another account, and it's going to require some travel, possibly even before the new year."

"You're going to miss New Year's Eve?"

"I hope not, but if I have to fly out to Tokyo, then I may not have a choice."

I try not to be sad about it, but I am. Being with him has brought me so much joy. He made me promises, and he's kept every one of them. I love him so much, and selfishly, I want to be with him.

However, our careers are what brought us together, and I know how much it means to him. If it were me who had to travel, I would want him to understand.

"We'll make it work," I promise.

He gives me a sweet kiss. "This is why I love you."

"Oh? Because of this *one* reason?" I say teasingly.

"This and many, many others."

I laugh. "Well, I am pretty fabulous."

"That you are."

"Now, let's get this tree fully decorated before our parents get here tomorrow."

We've barely had time to do anything Christmas related. Last night, three days before Christmas, we went and found a tree and threw some lights on it. Now we're doing our best not to make it look like total crap because I had the brilliant idea of hosting Christmas dinner this year.

As if I weren't already stressed out about seeing his mother again.

I groan, regretting my stupidity. "What?" he asks.

"I just . . . what if your mother still doesn't like me?"

Dean's brows furrow. "What are you talking about? She loves you."

"She loved me before we moved in together. She loved me when she thought this was just a fling and you'd move back to California instead of staying here."

Kayti Pritchard is the sweetest, most traditional mother who has ever lived.

When I flew out with him to California for Christmas the first year we were together, it was a shock for her, but she seemed happy to meet me. I guess Dean had talked about me to his family, which made me smile.

However, she wasn't happy when she caught us making out at midnight in the kitchen. After that, it was a little rocky, but we had been making progress. Then she put two and two together and realized we moved in together right after Christmas last year.

For two months, Dean would go in the bedroom, hiding any evidence that I moved into his apartment before she called him out. We endured three hours of listening to all the reasons we had to get married so we weren't living in sin, and how it was much too soon. I'm pretty sure she lived under the delusion that Dean was saving himself for marriage.

"I promise, she has no issues with you now."

I don't believe him.

"And you still want me to sleep in the guestroom while she's here?" I challenge.

He laughs. "No, that was a joke."

"Yeah right."

"This is our home, Holly. It's where we are building a life together. I love you, and regardless of whatever my mother says, that won't change. Now, let's not talk about mothers, dinner, or work, and enjoy what time we have instead."

I let out a deep sigh and wrap my arms around his middle. "I know what I would really like to do with the time we have before our parents arrive."

"What's that?"

I push up on my toes, moving my hands along his spine. "Well, first, I think we're overdressed."

His eyes soften and the mood around us shifts. "I think that can be remedied."

"Second, I think there will be a lot of touching . . . but where do we start . . ."

Dean leans down, scooping me up into his arms, and then his mouth is on mine, which saves me from having to elaborate.

## 6

# ▲ DEAN ▲

*I* love this woman. This crazy, exciting, maddening woman who came into my life, obliterating everything around her.

I carry her into our room, lying her on the bed like the goddess she is. Some days, I look at her and wonder what god I made happy enough for me to cross paths with her. Two years with her has taught me so much about love and life.

Holly is in a pair of leggings and a large green sweater than hangs off her shoulder, and she's never looked more beautiful. "You said something about clothes," I remind her as I start to unbutton my dress shirt.

She sits up, pulling her top off, showing a white lacy bra thing that hooks around her neck. The person who invented lace was a fucking genius. I stand here, hand suspended on a button, forgetting how to move.

"You're gorgeous."

"You're still dressed." Holly stands, her fingers finishing what mine can't. Each tug on my shirt does something to my heart. We never should've been, but fate stepped in and gave us a second chance.

One that I've vowed not to squander. There is no doubt in my mind that Holly is the answer to every prayer I've spoken. She's the other half to my soul, and I want to spend the rest of my life making her as happy as she's made me.

This Christmas is one she'll never forget.

I push her hair back off her face, thumb grazing her cheek. "How the hell did I ever catch you?"

She smiles. "I wonder the same thing. If that storm didn't happen, would we have each other?"

"I'd like to think so."

Holly rises up so her nose grazes mine. "I think we were meant to be."

I palm her breast and bring my lips to her neck. It doesn't matter that we've done this countless times. Each time with her is special.

She pushes my shirt off, her hands moving up my chest. "I love you."

"I love you," I reassure her. "So fucking much."

We move at the same time, fusing our lips together, giving ourselves over to the desire that pulses between us. I slide her leggings down, and she kicks them off before unbuttoning my pants.

As I watch her lie back on the bed, I take a second to appreciate what I'm lucky enough to have. I promised her that I would make her love Christmas again, and I've worked hard to give her happiness every day of the year, but this Christmas, I'm going all out.

I kiss down her neck and then her chest, sucking on her nipple the way she likes. Her fingers grip my hair as I go lower. I push her legs open, grazing the skin on her inner thigh.

"Dean," she moans.

My tongue darts out, just barely touching her clit, and she tightens her grip on my hair, pulling me where she wants me.

I lick, suck, and savor every sound that escapes her lips. Holly lifts her hips, and I start to fuck her with my mouth, bringing her closer and closer. I reach down and wrap my hand around my cock, moving in time with my tongue.

Holly explodes, her cries filling the room and then she's clawing at me to get near her.

"Please, Dean, I need you," she begs.

I love her voice, how needy she is for me. I climb

up, lining myself right where I want to be. Our gazes meet, and there's desire swimming in her brown eyes, but there is also love. So much love that if I were standing, I'd knock me to my knees.

The words that I want to say hover on my lips, but I have a plan and that doesn't include my saying it before making love to her.

Her hands cup my face as she studies me. "What is it?"

"You."

"I feel the same way."

She parts her legs a little more and shifts, urging me to enter her. "You're mine, Holly."

"Always."

I sink inside her, the warmth of her body wrapping around me like a blanket. I moan as she grips me, and then I make love to her, giving her everything I have.

"I'm FREAKING OUT." Holly is pacing at the exit from the terminal, shaking her hands as though she can expel the nervous energy. I try not to smile, but she's so damn cute. This is what she does before a pitch, and since we're in different departments, I never get to see this side of her anymore.

"Relax," I tell her, pulling her to my chest. "It'll be fine."

"I want your family to like me."

"And they do."

She gives me a skeptical side eye and then pushes away from me. "We should've gone there."

"Holly, stop, it'll be fine. My mother likes you, and she'll like you even more after she gets to know you better. Just . . . deep breaths."

This Christmas I have big plans. Everything is in motion, I just need our families to get here and do their part to make the surprise go off without issues.

My phone pings.

Mom: Deboarding now.

Me: Holly and I are here waiting for you.

Mom: Can't wait to see you.

I DON'T MISS that she didn't say *both* of you. I'm an only child, and after the loss of my father, she's become a bit overprotective. I think she believed I would move back to California after college, forgetting that she was the one who encouraged me to attend Northwestern, where I fell in love with the city and my job.

I take Holly's hand, standing as the people exit, passing the security desk. "I promise, this Christmas is going to be perfect."

Holly lets out a sigh, giving me a warm smile. "It already is."

I lean down, pressing my lips to hers. "Just be you, sweetheart. There's not a person who can resist you."

As I stare into those blue eyes, I hear someone clearing their throat.

Both our heads snap over. "Mom!"

"Dean, my sweet boy!"

I don't care that I'm thirty-four and a grown man, when my mother pulls me in for a hug, everything feels like it's possible. All the plans I've been agonizing over for the past few weeks, and even the stress of my mother coming, disappears.

It's going to be fine.

It has to be fine.

Mom releases me and smiles at Holly. "It's so good to see you," she says.

It's as though all the air that was being held in a balloon releases, and Holly hugs my mother. "I hope your flight was good."

"It was. Long, and really, you didn't need to

upgrade me." My mother pats my cheek. "But it was sweet."

"It was Holly's idea."

She turns to her. "Thank you, dear. It's great that Dean has someone to take care of him."

I want to argue with her, but then my phone rings. "It's the office, I have to take this," I say before excusing myself.

"Hi, Misty."

"Hey, Dean, sorry to bother you . . . I know you have the next four days off, but we have a big problem."

My assistant wouldn't call if it weren't something serious. "What's going on?"

She relays all the facts about the client and how they're getting ready to walk. I had everything shirred up before I left work on Friday.

"How did it get this bad?" I ask.

"It seems the client wasn't really on board from the beginning. Matthew has been trying to keep them happy, but . . . I guess they're a few hours away from cutting all ties with us. I . . ."

I look over at my mother and Holly. "I'll be in the office in forty minutes. No one touches anything."

And with that, all the stress I thought was gone, is back again.

## 7

"The apartment looks lovely," Dean's mother notes as she moves around. "And which is your room?"

Oh, I am going to kill him when he gets back. "Did you want to get unpacked?" I ask, hoping to avoid her question.

"No, no, it's fine. Do you know when Dean will be back?"

I shake my head. It's been three very long hours. At first, it was fine, we came home, put her bags in the spare room, and then went to the grocery store for provisions that I apparently missed. While I thought I got most of what I needed for our dinner tomorrow, Mrs. Pritchard wanted to make a few special dishes that her family eats each year that she didn't tell me about.

Then we called her mother, who won't be in until later tonight, but that phone call only gave me twenty minutes where I was not-so-patiently waiting for Dean to return.

Now, though, we were done adding a few decorations to the tree, final touches she thought would make it look a little more festive, and . . . still no Dean.

"I don't," I admit. "I'll text him."

My fingers fly over my phone, which hasn't left my hand, and I send a frantic text.

Me: Babe, where are you?

I KEEP STARING at the phone, willing it to respond. I look over at her with a smile. "He's probably dealing with the client."

She nods. "Does he do that a lot?"

"What do you mean?"

"I mean does he disappear often for work?"

"We are both very busy, and I understand it," I reassure her.

"He's always been this way." Her smile reaches her eyes. "As a child, he would be in his room, perfecting his papers as though each word had to be perfect. He could never quit until it was exactly the way he wanted it."

Mrs. Pritchard takes a seat on the couch, patting the cushion beside her. I make my way over, nerves starting to settle a bit. This kind of thing I could do. "He's still like that. I can't tell you how many nights I would wake up hearing the pounding of his fingers on the keyboard. It's why he's so successful at the company."

"I'm very proud of him."

"I am too."

We share a kinship here. "You love my son, don't you?"

"Very much."

"He is very much in love with you too."

I think back on the story of us, how if anyone else had been narrating it, we would've parted ways once the elevator opened. He would've gone to California, probably found a job and lived closer to his family. I wouldn't have gotten that promotion and would have lost out on the life I'm currently living. It's crazy how much can change in an instant.

Focusing on her, I do what maybe she's been waiting for from me. "Dean's happiness, his goals and dreams, are partially mine too. Loving him means sharing them, not wanting to diminish them."

"And if he got transferred?" She counters.

"Then we'd figure it out."

"I see the hesitation in your eyes. You're just as career focused as he is. That's what worries me sometimes."

I can understand that. She loves her son and doesn't want to see him hurt or held back. "And what if I got transferred? It's the same thing, we would find a way. I truly believe that. Dean and I . . . well, there's no one else for me."

Mrs. Pritchard takes my hand in both of hers. "Then hold on to each other, Holly. Don't let me or anyone else stand in your way. Life is short, so love him like tomorrow may not come."

My heart aches for her as a tear trickles down her cheek. She loved her husband so deeply, and even though it's been ten years, I can hear the pain in her voice.

"I will."

"When I lost my husband I remember wishing I hadn't fought him on the little things, you know?"

I nod. "My mother felt the same."

"Dean mentioned your father passed a few years ago."

"Yes, four."

"That must've been hard."

She has no idea. I was everything to my father. He doted on me, and I would've done anything to make him happy. We lost him so fast that there was no time to prepare. Not that anyone can ever really be ready, but he was fine one day and gone the next.

A massive heart attack.

A massive hole in my heart.

"It's been difficult, but my mother and I have wonderful memories."

She pats my hand. "The memories are what get us through, even on the holidays."

"And the people who are still alive."

Mrs. Pritchard smiles. "Yes, it's important to have family around us."

The holidays are bittersweet for me. I'm glad that I have Dean and people around me I love, but I miss my daddy. I think about all the things he'll never be a part of. He didn't get to meet Dean or see where we live. He'll never get to walk me down the aisle if I get married or hold my children. The holidays are a time I think about that loss more, yet I'm also happy for what I do have.

"I am really glad you came, Mrs. Pritchard."

"Oh, none of that. You're family now, you can call me Mom or Kayti."

I smile at her, wanting to cry. "Thank you, Mom."

She squeezes my hand. "No tears. We have a lot to do for this dinner. Come on, Holly, let's teach you how to make mashed potato pie. If you're going to host Christmas dinner from now on, you'll need to be sure it's always on the table. It's a Pritchard family tradition."

I fight back the sudden surge of emotions that come with her wanting to show me their family recipe. My lip trembles, and I force a smile. "Thank you."

She pats my back, her voice soothing. "It's me who should be thanking you, dear. You're what every mother hopes her son will find. Now, are you ready to get in the kitchen?"

I nod. "But first, can you tell me what the heck mashed potato pie is?"

"It's a dish best experienced." She winks and I wonder what the heck I got myself into.

"Where are you?" I ask into the receiver. "My mother got here an hour ago and you haven't called."

Dean let's out a heavy sigh. "What time is it?"

"Almost nine."

Seven hours have passed, and he's been completely silent. Not even responding to my texts. It wasn't until I emailed his assistant that he finally called me.

"Jesus. I . . . it's a shitshow here and I can't leave."

"What?"

"I'm sorry, Holls. I'm trying, but the client is in an uproar, and if I lose him—." He groans. "I can't even think about it."

I take a deep breath. "Can I help?"

"I wish you could, but . . . look it's bad and right now, I may have to fly out to do this in person. This is the big company I brought in and . . ."

He doesn't have to explain that if the client walks, he'll lose his job. I know if I were to assure him that if that happened—which I don't think it would—we'd be okay on my salary, he wouldn't change his mind.

Dean is driven, and its part of why I'm so attracted to him. He needs to fix this, not just because it's his job but because it matters to him.

"I understand. Listen, do whatever you have to, but Christmas is in two days."

"Believe me, sweetheart, I know."

"When would you leave?" I ask, feeling a slight tinge of disappointment at even the idea of him going.

"Tonight. Tomorrow. I don't know."

There's no mistaking the sadness in his voice. Even if I want to be mad, I can't be. Dean doesn't want to miss Christmas any more than I want him to.

"Okay, well, you tell me what you need, and we'll . . . we'll just have to adjust."

I start to make contingency plans because I won't let this ruin our holiday. It's important that this year goes off without any issues. The first year, everything was so new because we'd just survived being trapped in an elevator. But it was the holidays so it felt like some magical twist.

The next year, we had the most amazing time. And I knew. I knew that Dean was everything.

He means presents under the tree, dinner with family, snow, and smiles—not work disasters in Tokyo.

However, like I told his mother, I love him. A single day doesn't have to define a lifetime. We'll find a way to salvage Christmas.

## 8

# ▲ Dean ▲

It's two in the morning on Christmas Eve, and I'm still at my desk. Nothing is going right. I don't know where the hell this deal fell off the rails, but no matter what I do, it won't go on track.

The two owners are talking to each other over the video chat.

I rub my eyes, exhausted and beyond frustrated. This was supposed to be the deal that set the entire new year off for my team. We were gaining a new brand that would launch multiple products through us.

I had this done.

And now it's slipping through my fingers.

I drain the remainder of my coffee, praying this

caffeine will kick in, and then look at the photo of Holly and I on my desk.

She's smiling up at me, her hand resting on my chest as my lips rest on her forehead while the colored lights of the tree shine behind us. It was our first official Christmas as a couple. Last year, after we went to California to see my mom and then had Christmas with her mother, I surprised her with a trip to New York City.

It didn't matter that the holiday was over, we went to see the tree, saw a Broadway play, and walked around Central Park hand in hand.

My client returns. "We would like another meeting," he requests.

"Can you give me a few days? Let's get through the holiday and regroup."

"I will discuss it with the owners and let you know in a few hours."

That's the best I can ask for. "Flights are limited, Jon," I remind him. "I won't be able to get out until after the holiday, just know that."

He nods. "I understand."

I will beg, borrow, and steal not to have my plans thwarted. Everything was supposed to be set in motion last night, but I got stuck here.

"Thank you. Send me an email, it's late and I need to get some rest."

"Thank you, Dean. I'll be in touch."

And with that, I close my laptop and head home, trying to get my thoughts arranged on how to still have it all come together.

"DEAN? BABY, WAKE UP," Holly's soft voice calls me from the edge of consciousness. I feel her fingers rake through my hair.

My eyes open, and I find the woman I love staring down at me. "Hey."

"Hi."

"Come here," I say, making room for her to snuggle beside me. "I'm sorry about dinner."

Holly gets comfortable. "It was fine. Our mothers are now best friends, and I was able to spend some much-needed time with them. It was nice, and it worked out. How did the meetings go?"

I tuck my one arm up under my head, running my other hand against Holly's spine. "Not well. I don't know where the hell it went crazy, but . . . I'm pretty sure I'm going to be heading out there."

"I'm sorry."

"It's the job, right?"

She chuckles softly. "It's definitely what we deal

with now. Remember when our biggest issue was the pitch?"

"Remember how I kicked your ass so many times?"

Holly lifts her head, looking up at me. "I think you're confused."

"Who got the account when we battled?" I ask with my brow raised.

"You only got it because I ended up skipping my pitch to go to California."

"Ahh. I remember that now."

Holly shakes her head. "I don't know what I'm going to do with you."

I stare at her, my heart in my throat because this isn't how I planned it. While everything was supposed to be special and perfect last night, for some reason, this moment feels . . . right.

"Marry me," I say and shift to sit up, taking her hands in mine. "Marry me, Holly. That's what I want you to do with me. I love you. I had this grand plan to propose last night, and then I was going to do it tonight. But you're here, looking at me, and I can't . . . I can't think of anything else. I want to be your husband, and I probably shouldn't have done it like this, but—"

Her hand touches my lips, silencing me. "Did

anyone ever tell you that you talk too much?" Tears fill her eyes, and she smiles. "Yes."

"Yes?"

A lone tear falls down her cheek. "Yes."

I take her face in my hands, bringing our mouths together. It's a mix of tears and smiling as the moment settles around us.

"I have something for you." I shift away from her just long enough to grab the ring out of the bottom of my side table. I lift the lid, revealing the ring I had made.

She gasps. "Dean . . ."

"I wanted it to be Christmas all year."

There, in the box is a large marquise cut solitaire diamond and, on each side, there are three small stones. One ruby and two emeralds, making it look like holly leaves.

I lift the ring, placing it on her finger. "It's beautiful. It's . . . it's perfect."

"You're perfect."

She kisses me again and then pulls back to look at her hand. Now to ensure the rest of my plan actually happens.

## 9

"**We're** engaged!" I yell as Dean and I emerge from the bedroom.

Our mothers rise from the couch and rush toward us. "You did it!" His mother's grin is wide as she reaches us first. "I'm so happy for you both. Now, God won't be upset about you living in sin."

I want to laugh because it's not like we're married, we're just engaged, but I won't ruin her mood. It's Christmas Eve, and she's happy.

My mother pulls me into her arms. "Oh, my sweet girl. I couldn't be any happier."

She loves Dean because he's a great guy who works hard and treats me well but she also wants grandkids and this brings her one step closer to getting them.

"Thank you."

"Your father would be so happy too," she says a little misty eyed.

"I wish he were here."

Her hand rests on my cheek. "Me too, baby. But he's here. I feel him all around us this year."

"Tomorrow is going to be so special," his mother says while pressing her hands together. "So special. I just know that it'll all be magical."

Dean gives her a strange look. "Yes, because it's Christmas."

"That's what I mean. Christmas for you two especially is extra magical."

There's a niggling sense that I'm missing something. My mother grabs my hand, pulling me toward her. "How did he propose?"

"He just kind of said it. I know it doesn't sound amazing or romantic, but it was. We were just lying there, smiling, and he asked me to marry him."

"I think that's perfect for you, Holly. You've never needed anything big."

I haven't. I like low-key when it comes to things like this. Honestly, I would be completely happy with just these people and maybe my best friend, Chelle, at our wedding. As happy as I am about all of this, there is a brief second of sadness when I realize my dad won't be here to walk me down the aisle.

There won't be a father-daughter dance. It'll just be me.

I push the thought from my head, this is a special day. I'm engaged to the most wonderful man in the world.

Dean comes behind me, wrapping his arms around my middle. "Are you happy?"

"Blissfully."

"How is this year's Christmas in comparison? Are you starting to agree that this is the most wonderful time of the year yet?"

I smile, tilting my head back to look at him. "Most definitely."

"Good, and we still have tomorrow."

He leans down, giving me a sweet kiss. "I love you."

"I love you, too."

Our mothers are clucking like hens about what to cook, what to wear, and something else I don't catch.

"They're fast friends," Dean notes while holding me tight.

"Thank God. They're all we have."

He laughs and then groans. "As much as I don't want to, I need to check my email and figure out what's going on with my client. If I have to leave, there will be very little time to prepare."

His mother bristles. "Now? It's Christmas Eve and

we have a big dinner planned. Not to mention, you wanted to take us downtown."

"I wish I didn't have to, Mom, but . . . I can't neglect this."

She sighs with a hint of frustration. "Are you sure you want to marry my son, Holly? A workaholic who can't put the computer down—not even for the holidays."

I laugh and look at him. "There's no one else I'd rather be with."

She humphs and mutters under her breath as she walks into the kitchen.

"I'm sorry," he says.

"I understand. If this were my big client, I would need to do the same thing."

While it's Christmas and I wish he weren't stuck working, I get it. I hoped this year we'd be doing things together, but I have tomorrow with him, and with my mother here, it's not so bad.

He kisses my temple. "Thank you. I promise, I'll make it all up to you tomorrow."

I grin. "Well, we could always be very quiet tonight."

Dean winks. "I look forward to testing that."

He heads back into the bedroom, and I go help in the kitchen—and by help, I mean I stand around aimlessly while they fuss over it all. We're having ham, mashed potato pie (which is basically twice baked potatoes but much more complicated), green beans, and my mother's famous Pierniki, which is a polish gingerbread.

Mom calls me over. "Here, you knead the dough, but not too much."

I've done this every year since I was three. My great-grandma taught my grandma and then she taught my mother and she taught me.

"Isn't this wonderful?" Mrs. Pritchard asks. "*This* is what the holidays are about, it's family and love."

My mother nods. "I was so worried that Holly would end up alone after that last guy she was with."

"Could we not?" I ask. "I got engaged today, and I'd like to only think of Dean."

"Of course, sweetheart. Dean is a good man. You're lucky he caught you."

I smile, thinking back on that elevator debacle. "I was lucky."

Mrs. Pritchard waves her hand. "It was fate."

"I think it was a Christmas miracle," I say as I remember looking up at the mistletoe that was hanging above us.

This year, I made sure I hung it in our bedroom, which he was more than happy to take advantage of.

After a few more minutes, Dean enters, and the look on his face says it all. "You lost it?"

"No, but I have to leave for Tokyo."

"When?"

He closes his eyes. "I don't know, but I should be getting on a plane right now."

"Dean, it's Christmas," his mother says.

When he looks back at me, I can see the regret. "I know. Believe me and . . . God!" he yells in frustration. "I had it all planned."

His mother walks over, and places a hand on his shoulder. "Nothing is ever broken that can't be fixed. We'll . . . well, we'll do it today."

"Do what?" I ask.

Dean comes in front of me, his hands taking mine. "I had a plan. When I asked you to marry me, that was only part of it."

I blink a few times, not really sure what the heck else there is to it. "Okay . . ."

"See, I made a promise to you in that elevator. I promised that Christmas would be your favorite time again. I wanted to make you love it again."

"You have," I assure him.

"I want every memory from this year on to be filled with joy, Holly. I want you to think of us—of all we've shared and all that's still to come."

"Dean, you're not ruining Christmas by going away. It's a day. A single day in the expanse of our lives together. I love you, and I know that you're not leaving because you want to."

He shakes his head. "If I have to get on a plane tomorrow, then we're going to make this happen today." There's so much determination in his voice that I don't know how to respond. "Go into the bedroom, and don't come out until I get you, okay?"

"Uhh, okay?"

He kisses me, ignoring that our mothers are standing right there, and then turns me. "Go. I have a lot of work to do."

## ▲ Dean ▲

*I* call the maintenance worker, Nick, who pried us out of that elevator. "Dean? Is everything still set for tomorrow?" he asks.

"Actually, no. I have an issue and need to see if you can get here today."

"Today? You're going to get married today?"

"Yes, I have to go out of town unexpectedly."

He makes a few noises as though he's moving around. "I guess I can. When do you need me?"

"Three hours?"

"Snow is coming down pretty bad, but I'll get there. Don't you worry. I won't leave you stranded."

I laugh because he's who saved us last time, and it seems that, once again, a bit of snow and some luck is going to save this holiday season.

"I'll let you know where we're having it since all my plans are being changed."

"All right. I'll see you later today."

We hang up, and I go in where both our mothers are. "Okay, Charlie will be here, what else do we need to get done?"

"I called the florist," Holly's mother informs us. "She can deliver wherever we need her to in the next hour. She was already done with everything."

"Okay." I turn to my mother. "Well, then I need a venue."

I call the restaurant I reserved for tomorrow that overlooks the lake. It's magical when the navy pier is lit up and everything is covered in snow, so it would've been . . . perfect. However, they explain that they can't accommodate a spur-of-the moment wedding, even if it's only six people. Me, Holly, my mother and hers makes four.

Shit. I need to text Holly's best friend, Chelle, and my best man, Brian.

Me: I know this is last minute, but can you come now?

Chelle: Now? For what?

Me: I have to leave for Tokyo, so we're going to do this now.

Chelle: Oh! Okay! I'll head over.

She only lives a few blocks away, so that won't be an issue.

Next to tell Brian, who was going to head to the bar with the girl he was banging last year. They have some weird pact, and . . . well, he's a damn mess.

Me: Please tell me you're sober and not hooking up with your ex or whatever the hell you call this girl.

Brian: What's wrong?

Me: I'm getting married today, and I need you to get here.

Brian: I thought it was tomorrow.

Me: Change of plans.

Brian: I'll be there in an hour.

THERE'S something I'm forgetting.

"The cake."

My mother smiles. "Don't you worry about that. Give Meredith and I two hours and we'll have a cake done."

Holly's mother smiles. "Kayti and I will handle it. You get yourself ready."

"Where do we do this?" I ask. "I can't get the restaurant today, which means no food. Shit."

"Dean, we have a feast here."

"She's going to hate this."

Her mother shakes her head. "You're planning a wedding for a Christmas gift. She will not hate a single thing."

I really freaking hope not. When I came up with this, it all sounded good. It was a no fuss, easy wedding without any of the stress. She has been so busy and it wasn't about a wedding for me, it's about the marriage. I want to start our lives together—easy and low maintenance.

I wanted stress free, but now it's a fucking mess.

I try to think of other venue options and then it hits me.

The place I took her on our first real date: the museum.

And I happen to have a connection. I text Chelle.

Me: Can have the wedding at the museum?

Chelle: We're closed now, but I can call my boss and ask.

Me: Okay, let me know.

AFTER A FEW MINUTES she texts me back.

Chelle: We're good. They just said I have to make sure it's cleaned up. I'll text you details to have things delivered without anyone seeing and all that.

Me: You're a lifesaver.

I LET everyone know where to meet, which actually works out perfectly. Now, I can have something special for Holly.

With a plan in place, I head into the bedroom and find her lying on the bed with her ereader.

"Reading anything good?"

She smiles. "Well, the hero just told the heroine how special she is and how he wouldn't want to live another day without her. It was so sweet."

"Well, I think you're special, and I don't want to live a day without you."

"You make the perfect book boyfriend."

"What the hell is a book boyfriend?" I ask.

"You wouldn't understand because they don't exist in real life, no matter how much we all wish they did."

I roll my eyes. "Listen, I know tomorrow isn't exactly going as planned, but how about we salvage today?"

"What are you up to?" Holly's voice is layered with skepticism.

"Nothing, I just want to try to have some of my surprise still happen."

She eyes me with curiosity. "All right."

All right. I may actually pull this off.

WE GET to the Museum of Contemporary Art about two hours later, and I feel as if this all might be okay. I stalled as much as I could, giving our mothers time to get the cake out of the oven and the food almost done. That also gave Brian and Chelle time to get the flowers and everything else here at least.

There is something magical about this place. Even though we've been here a hundred times, I always feel like it's new and exciting. Getting married here is truly going to be perfect.

"I love this place," she says, mirroring my thoughts.

"Me too."

"It's where you told me you loved me the first time."

I grin. "I remember."

Holly's hands are wrapped around my arm as we move through the building. "Did Chelle open up for us?"

I laugh. "She did. It's what took me a while, I needed to get everything set."

"It's a good thing we have friends in high places."

We walk through the exhibits, looking at some new things when my phone pings with a text from Chelle, telling me that everything is set and where to bring her to get ready.

"How about we go this way?" I suggest.

"But we always go see the contemporary paintings next."

I give her a wry smile. "Let's try something new."

"What are you up to Dean Pritchard?" She asks, tilting her head at me.

"You'll see."

We make our way down a few halls until we're in the new section that has a large sculpture in the center.

"Chelle!" Holly yells and then rushes to her. "What the hell are you wearing a ball gown for?"

Chelle, who is wearing a burgundy dress, looks over at me and smiles. "Your dress is hanging in the other room."

"My dress for what?" She takes a step back, looking between us.

I go to her and drop to one knee. "When I asked you to marry me, I had this elaborate plan to make it special. See, I planned to ask you while we were at what I planned to be our wedding."

"What?"

"Marry me today, Holly. Marry me here, in the place that means so much to us. Marry me in front of our friends. Right now." Tears fill her eyes as my mother, her mother, and Brian step out, all dressed in formal attire. "Marry me on Christmas Eve."

She sniffles and then drops down to me. "You planned our wedding?"

"I know you didn't want a big wedding, and Christmas means everything to us."

"It does. And you mean everything to me, you sweet, wonderful, amazing man."

"Chelle has a dress, all you have to do is agree."

She looks around as tears fall. "But who is going to marry us?"

Then Charlie walks through the door. "Did someone need help getting hitched for Christmas? I happen to be ordained."

Holly's laughter erupts through her soft sob. "You . . . you . . . God, I can't even speak. You did all this. For me?"

"I'd do anything for you."

She launches forward, knocking me back to the ground as she holds me tight. "You're the best thing that ever happened to me."

I smile up at her. "So, you'll marry me today?"

"I'd marry you any day."

# Holly

Chelle is behind me, checking over my hair and makeup. "You look perfect."

"Even after the tears?"

"Yes, even after crying. You truly look gorgeous. Ready for the dress?"

God, he even got a dress? This is insane. The amount of time and preparation he went through is crazy. "How did he pull this off?"

"It was supposed to be tomorrow at a place by the lake, but . . . we improvised."

"He was that sure I would say yes."

"Of course, he was. Dean loves you more than any man I've ever seen, and you love him just as much. Not a single one of us thought you would say no."

I am so lucky. Everything about this, even though

he planned it just a few hours ago to be here is perfect. Well, not that I've seen anything other than the people around us. As soon as I said yes, Chelle and the mothers took me into this room to get ready. My blonde hair is curled, falling down my back and my makeup looks like a professional did it, thanks to Chelle's ridiculous hours spent on YouTube.

"I just can't believe he planned a wedding." She smiles and then jerks her head to the long white garment bag. "That's it?"

"Now, I will say, he did not pick this out. He enlisted help, and your mother and I found what we thought you'd want."

I look at her with a mix of curiosity and appreciation. "Is this why you had me looking at dresses online?"

"Maybe."

Chelle said something about a wedding exhibit here and asked for my help finding dresses. The anticipation is too much as I practically run toward the bag, but I pull the zipper down carefully.

"Oh my God!"

"Don't cry, Holly!" she warns.

I bite my tongue and fan my eyes to try to stop. It's *the* dress. The one that I couldn't tear my eyes away from as we searched the web. It's a long, lace dress with a small train that flares out softly, but it's the top of the dress that is stunning. There are thin satin straps that hang off the shoulder, they're not really for support, but just because it's pretty and the top of the dress is tight against the body with a sweetheart neckline.

"It's perfect."

My mother comes up behind me. "It's you."

I nod, still not able to take my eyes away.

Then I remember how much it cost, and I gasp. "No, it's too expensive."

"Holly, your father and I saved an exorbitant amount of money for your education, and then you were so damn smart you got a full ride to college. Believe me, he would've wanted me to use this money on your wedding."

"Mom . . ."

"No." She lifts her hands to stop me. "I won't cry yet. We are going to take photos, and I won't be smudgy."

I smile and pull her in for a hug. "I love you."

"Same, peanut." She uses the name my father gave me when I was little.

"I wish he was here," I say, unable to stop myself.

"I know, but he would've loved this. A man who takes this much time for a woman he loves is a special one. What you and Dean share is something that I only dreamed you would find."

And I did find it. I found love in an elevator of all places with a man I thought I could never forgive. While it wasn't perfect, everything that has happened since has been. He is truly the other half to my soul.

"Thank you, guys. Thank you for all of this."

Chelle comes forward. "Let's get you into this dress."

With the help of the people I love, I get in it, and . . . I can't even think about how I feel. It's too much.

Nerves fill me, and I start to shake out my hands. "I'm ready."

"You look absolutely stunning," Chelle says as she winks. "I'll see you out there."

Then Dean's mother approaches. "I couldn't be any happier that you will be my daughter."

I fight back the tears, and she dabs at her eyes.

Now it's my mother "Will you walk me out to him?"

Her lips tremble. "Oh, Holly, nothing would make me happier."

A tear falls down each of our cheeks, and we giggle as both reach to wipe the other's cheek dry.

"Ready?"

"Yes. I'm ready."

My mother and I walk out and down the hall to the room that I would know with my eyes closed. It's our room. The one with photographs of eyes and lips all around it. The individual pieces of the exhibit come together in the middle, making the parts appear to be one face.

Dean and I always felt like this was what we were—two parts that, when put together, became whole.

It's the room where he told me he loved me.

However, it's been transformed. There's a wooden arch at the back of the room that has holly leaves and berries wrapped around it. All around the room are poinsettia plants, and garland. It's green and red and lush and it's a lot of holly.

We walk toward him, as he stands there, arms folded in front of him, standing so tall and trying not to cry, but I have no chance of holding it back.

I smile at him and he smiles back.

When we reach him, his eyes are watery and he's slowly shaking his head. "You're so beautiful, you take my breath away."

"You did all this?"

"I had help from some elves."

I grin. "This is a lot of holly."

Dean's fingers gently grip my chin. "There's never too much Holly."

Charlie clears his throat, and I can't help but want to laugh at all of this. He's the same as he was the first time I met him with his long white beard with reddened cheeks. Here we are, on Christmas Eve being married by a man who looks like Santa.

"Are you ready to marry me?"

"I was ready the day of the elevator."

He laughs and then turns to Charlie. "Okay."

"Dean?" I say as a thought comes. "How? I mean, is this . . . legal?"

I can see the discomfort before he takes both my hands in his. "We're married where it matters, here, around our family and friends. I couldn't find a way to get a marriage license without your consent."

"Well, that's comforting."

He laughs. "But I wanted our anniversary to be Christmas. I wanted to surprise you and take all the stress away. This will always be the day you became my wife, but next week, we'll go downtown and sign it to make it legal."

"Just when I think I can't love you anymore than I do, you say the right thing."

"Let me say even more."

I nod. "Marry me today."

"Nothing could stop me."

We both turn to Charlie, and he begins. We exchange rings, and then it's time for the vows. I haven't had more than an hour to process this, but instead of feeling uneasy, it's as though I feel even calmer than ever.

"Dean . . ." Charlie prompts.

"Two years ago, I almost lost you—or maybe it was that I wasn't sure I could even have you, but then, a snowstorm like we're having today allowed me the opportunity to fix all that. When I think of my life without you, it's colorless and bland. It's filled with dark nights and sunless skies. You are what brings meaning to my world. You're the most precious thing to me, Holly. I told you that I would make you love Christmas again, but I want to give you every holiday and every day in between. I promise that I will love you, cherish you, and never forsake you. You are my love, my heart, and my soul."

Tears fall down my cheek and I barely hear Charlie say my name.

"Dean, you are my Christmas. You're the joy and the hope that comes with it. You're the miracle I don't know how I was fortunate enough to receive. I was lost that day in the elevator, feeling like nothing good could ever come again, but there you were. While we may not have been brave enough had it not been for that, I think my heart was always meant to find you and that we'd be here somehow. There is not another person who could love me the way that you do. I promise to understand you, love you, and be there no matter what comes our way. Today, I pledge my fidelity and my soul to you."

There are sniffles around the room as Dean takes my face in his hands before turning to Charlie. "I'm going to kiss her now," he explains.

He points up to the mistletoe above us. "It's bad luck not to."

His lips touch mine in the most wonderful kiss that has ever been.

"Merry Christmas, wife."

I grin back at him. "Merry Christmas, husband."

He lifts me into his arms, carrying me back down the aisle, and I know that Christmas will always be the best holiday that ever was. All because of him.

**What is really THE END ... well, who knows next year I may go crazy again. But at least for now, let's go with it**

*I really hope you enjoyed this sugary sweet and romantic Christmas story. I had a lot of fun writing it during a time when it sort of felt like everything was just ... well, you know. We're all living it.*

*Because this is TRULY my favorite time of year, I wanted to give you yet another gift. Last year, Melanie Harlow and I wrote the cutest holiday story that we laughed and smiled the entire time writing. If you flip to the next page, you'll be able to download it FREE if you sign up for our newsletter!*

If you're on Facebook, join my private reader group for special updates and a lot of fun.

Corinne Michaels Books Facebook Group:

→http://on.fb.me/1tDZ8Sb

# FREE BOOK

Dear Reader,

I hope you enjoyed this Christmas short story. I have to tell you, I loved writing it. There was something so fun about just enjoying a good love story around the holidays. (Let's just blame it on my obsession with Hallmark movies).

Last year, Melanie Harlow and I wrote the most cheesy and fun holiday story together. If you didn't get a chance to read *Baby, it's Cold Outside* in the *Christmas in the City* anthology, we'd like to offer it to you free when you sign up for our newsletter.

GRAB IT HERE:

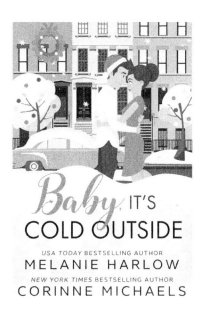

https://BookHip.com/GCQHBW

# KEEP UP WITH CORINNE

If you'd like to just keep up with my sales and new releases, you can follow me on BookBub or sign up for text alerts!

BookBub: https://www.bookbub.com/authors/corinne-michaels

Text Alerts: Text cmbooks to 77948

Not Until You

If I Only Knew

**The Arrowood Brothers**

Come Back for Me

Fight for Me

The One for Me

Stay for Me

**Willow Creek Valley Series (Coming 2021)**

Return to Us

One Chance for Us

A Moment for Us

Could Have Been Us

**Co-Write with Melanie Harlow**

Hold You Close

Imperfect Match

**Standalone Novels**

All I Ask

## ACKNOWLEDGMENTS

To my husband and children. You sacrifice so much for me to continue to live out my dream. Days and nights of me being absent even when I'm here. I'm working on it. I promise. I love you more than my own life.

My readers. There's no way I can thank you enough. It still blows me away that you read my words. You guys have become a part of my heart and soul.

My beta reader Melissa Saneholtz: I don't even know what to say at this point. It's been almost 20 books and you haven't killed me yet, for that, you get a cookie.

Chelle Bliss: thank you this insanely amazing cover. Seriously, I don't even know what to say that can adequately thank you for it. I am so blessed to call you a friend.

My assistant, Christy Peckham: How many times can one person be fired and keep coming back? I think we're running out of times. No, but for real, I couldn't imagine my life without you. You're a pain in my ass but it's because of you that I haven't fallen apart.

Melanie Harlow, thank you for being the Glinda to my Elphaba or Ethel to my Lucy. Your friendship means the world to me and I love writing with you. I feel so blessed to have you in my life.

To Passionflix, thank you for taking my words and making it into a film. It was a dream that I truly never thought would happen. Thank you to everyone that was onset, including the actors who did SO good bringing this to life.

Mindi, thank you for being in L.A. with me during it all. I will never forget that trip (including my meltdown), but you were my rock.

Vi Keeland, you are truly one of the most wonderful and special friends I have. Thank you for asking me to be in this anthology two years ago. If it weren't for you, I never would've written this story.

Zoom Authors, each morning I wake up, ready to tackle the words because of you. Seriously, you'll never know how much you save me each day. I don't know that I could've done any of this story or the other if it weren't for you.

Bait, Crew, and Corinne Michaels Books—I love you more than you'll ever know.

My agent, Kimberly Brower, I am so happy to have you on my team. Thank you for your guidance and support.

Melissa Erickson, you're amazing. I love your face. Thank you for always talking me off the ledge that is mighty high.

I want to thank everyone who make my holidays so special. I couldn't do this without my farmers and hens. Each year we snuggle up and you remind me how lucky I am to have you in my life.

# ABOUT THE AUTHOR

Corinne Michaels is a *New York Times, USA Today, and Wall Street Journal* bestselling author of romance novels. Her stories are chock full of emotion, humor, and unrelenting love, and she enjoys putting her characters through intense heartbreak before finding a way to heal them through their struggles.

Corinne is a former Navy wife and happily married to the man of her dreams. She began her writing career after spending months away from her husband while he was deployed—reading and writing were her escape from the loneliness. Corinne now lives in Virginia with her husband and is the emotional, witty, sarcastic, and fun-loving mom of two beautiful children.

Printed in Great Britain
by Amazon